Love and Nothing Else
Readings for Writers volume 2
12 more essays on short stories and their writers

Mike Smith

Copyright © 2016 Mike Smith

All rights reserved.

ISBN:1530677750
ISBN-13:9781530677757

DEDICATION

To the writers of the Facets of Fiction Writers Workshop

CONTENTS

	Acknowledgments	i
1	Stacy Aumonier	1
2	L.A.G. Strong	9
3	Elizabeth Bowen	13
4	M.R.James	20
5	Marc le Goupils	24
6	Prosper Merimee	29
7	Margaret Oliphant	37
8	A.E.Coppard	41
9	Vladimir Korolenko	46
10	Francois Coppee	51
11	Michael de Larrabeiti	57
12	Arthur Miller	61

ACKNOWLEDGMENTS

Several of these essays have appeared on the Thresholds website and on BHDandMe's blog

1 A LITTERY AND EDDICATED MAN
'A MAN OF LETTRS' BY STACY AUMONIER

I recognise something going on in Aumonier's stories. In the couple of dozen I've read, there seems often to be an attempt to solve a problem of 'telling.' In particular I saw it in *A Man of Letters*. This is what might be called an epistolary story: one constructed out of letters. It's a form associated with the novel, and can produce a very tedious story if not handled well.

Aumonier's handling is deft, and he sets himself a difficult task, because his eponymous hero is a working class chap with atrocious spelling and a weak grasp on language. This element alone presents the author with lots of difficulties; how to present his hero without sending him up, not the least. Aumonier is a comic writer, but our laughter must be sympathetic. We are not to laugh at Alf Codling, but at his situation. (I should point out that I'm being careful with my spelling – especially when copying out the quotations.)

'When you was on sentry go in the dessert at night it was so quiet and missterius.'

Intentional misspellings in English literature go back a long way – consider Mrs Malaprop, who bequeathed her name to what has become a literary technique – and so does the depiction of the uneducated as manglers of the language. Shakespeare could give us a laugh at characters like the door-keeper in Macbeth, or the rustic thespians in A Midsummer Night's Dream., but he also put profound thoughts into their, and our, seemingly shallow heads.

Alf's first letter opens with some poor English, but, piquing the difference between form and content – something that should interest us as writers of fiction – what the words are about eclipses how they are used:

'My Dear Annie,

I got into an awful funny mood lately.'

He tells her that she'll think him 'barmy,' but will we?

'It started I think when I was in Egypt. Nearly all us chaps who was out there felt it a bit.'

The chaps who had been 'out there' – in World War One - will have been among Aumonier's readers, I suspect, and even those of us who were not, might have an inkling of what he is recalling. A few missing commas, a verb-subject mismatch and a questionable pronoun do not a moron make.

Aumonier is not seeking to ridicule his character, but to show him writing conversationally, and therefore, as a normal rather than a formal person. He is also showing him as a man struggling to push the envelope of his own awareness, both of the world and of himself. Uneducated he might be, but self-educating he most certainly is.

'I want to be good for you and I want to know all about things and that.'

If 'things and that' is shorthand for all that we do not yet have the words for, then here is a serious aspiration, comically expressed; and look at his motivation. He wishes to better himself, not for simple 'self improvement', but 'for you.'

The opening line of the second letter, addressed to James Weeks, who runs the local literary society offers another opportunity for comedy, and a comedy that could satirize either reader or writer, and, in fact, both.

'Someone tells me you are a littery society'

How Weeks responds to this will reveal him as clearly as his own letter has revealed Alf. The story has a short cadenza here, for Weeks is away, and the letter must be passed on, as Alf is informed in a rather pompous note from Week's secretary. This serves to raise our expectation of how his query will be treated, but before that we must get a reply from Annie.

That the story is about Alf and his attempts to educate himself, and to deal with his des(s)ert experiences should not distract us from the fact that it is also a story about the relationship between Alf and Annie. After all, it is 'to be good for you,' that he wants to become more fully himself.

Annie's letter gives us the context for his aspiration. She is no upwardly mobile snob seeking to aspirate his haitches and to eradicate his accent.

'My Dear Alf,

You are a dear old funny old bean.'

Her English is no better than his, but her thoughts are simpler, and more accepting, but then she has not been alone in the desert, and at war. She wants to help, but her grasp of what he is looking for is weak.

'I can lend you some books. Cook is a great reader.'

A couple of (presumably) light novelists are mentioned, in stark contrast to the list that Weeks hits Alf with a little later in the tale.

'Jevons' *Primer of Logic*

Welton's *Manual of Logic*

Brackenbury's *Primer of Psychology* ...and more!

By the time we get to this list, however, we are fairly sure that Weeks, far from ridiculing Alf by the suggestion, is genuinely trying to help him: 'Do not be discouraged!' he writes.

In fact, Weeks is an important character in this story. He represents not only the 'littery society' in particular, but that wider literary society that those of us who read – and write - belong to. His reaction to Alf is critical to what sort of story this is, and who, and what it is about.

His first response to Alf is as formal as his secretary's has been, and asks for 'qualifications,' which, by this part of the story, we are sure that Alf does not have. Aumonier is testing our prejudices here, and perhaps our characters too. We have the chance to laugh maliciously if we wish, or perhaps laughter is not a matter choice, but of pre-disposition?

Weeks receives a reply that reveals Alf more fully to him:

'I am not what you might call a littery or eddicated man at all.'

But in the same letter Alf has revealed what he has already told to Annie, and he makes a suggestion to Weeks:

'Perhaps sir you have to have been throw it if you know what I mean.'

And Weeks, perhaps does know, for he writes inviting Alf to join, and then goes about finding a seconder for the proposed membership. Here is the first opportunity for Aumonier to show us Weeks from another angle, that which he shows to his friend Samuel Childers.

'He sounds the kind of person who would make a splendid foil to old Baldwin with his tortuous metaphysics.'

The fact that this reply is to some extent equivocal, raises the story from a level at which it might have operated. There is an ambiguity here about just how sincere Weeks is in his acceptance. To what extent has he understood, and respected Alf? To what extent does he see him as an amusing goad to a pompous fellow member? This ambiguity allows Weeks too, to be taken on a journey of self discovery, and perhaps of self improvement, and depending on our perceptions, and on our points of view, it is a journey on which we might accompany him.

Childers, in his written reply thinks 'you mean it as a joke.' Weeks, we shall discover, is better than that, though.

Annie, however, is nearer to Childers, thinking that Alf does not need to change, fearing perhaps that he will move away from her if he does.

'I shouldn't think the littery society much cop myself.'

The letters pass between Annie and Alph – that was a genuine Freudian spelling error, so I'll leave it in - and Alf, and between Alf and the organiser of the Society, and between the organiser and various members. There are so many possible stereotypical ambushes here, but Aumonier avoids them all, for it is not merely a matter of him bashing one class of person or another – with one possible exception that I shall note later. He is creating individuals in a feasible situation, who have 'expected' attitudes, but who do not become caricatures. Weeks' letter to Childers has been unambiguous.

'We must certainly get Alfred Codling into our society.'

Weeks is no fool. He know that Alf is uneducated and inarticulate, and he does have an agenda, but it is not to make a fool of him. Alf goes along, hopelessly out of his depth. Weeks lends him books, and the evening comes when Baldwin delivers a paper. Alf cannot contain himself, but neither can he express his objections, and leaves the meeting having 'insulted' the man.

'To my amazement my ex-lance-corporal rose heavily to his feet. His face was brick red and his eyes glowed with anger.'

The Society disintegrates in the aftermath of this event, as letters pass between the insulted, the outraged, and Weeks and his ally! And all this, expressed, and told, in the letters. A letter from Sam's daughter to a friend allows an oblique look at the situation, and at Alf.

'I have been to two of the meetings especially to observe the mechanic with the soul. He is really quite a dear.'

That her comic quip 'the mechanic with the soul' is, on another level, an exact description of Alf, and not at all comic, should not be lost on us; comic irony with serious intent.

One letter in particular is crucial, to the story, and to our acceptance of the story, and that is the one in which Alf explains to Weeks why he was so rude. I think it's rather a masterpiece of writing, because within it, using Alf's still inarticulate and uneducated voice, Aumonier manages to explain, and to tell us about Alf's epiphany in the desert. Weeks, whom it would have been so easy to pass off as a bigoted abuser of Alf, is presented as a man of understanding and true education. His resignation precipitates the disintegration of the group, but he resigns in support of Alf's action, and continues to support his protégé in other ways.

Aumonier is a comic writer, and one with a light touch. None of these characters are stereotypes, except perhaps for the villain Baldwin. His letter to Weeks, complaining about the acceptance of Alf into the group, puts forward some arguments, about literature and what it means to us, as individuals and in the wider society.

> 'he may be a very good young man in his place. But why join a literary society? Surely we want to raise the intellectual standard of the society, not lower it?'

The club secretary, writing to Baldwin, supports his opinions.

> 'We might as well admit agricultural labourers, burglars, grooms and barmaids, and the derelicts of the town.'

Baldwin, in his letter of resignation late in the story includes an OBE in his signature, something that Aumonier, we must remember, has awarded him, and in doing so he also has awarded that medal, and the establishment it implies, the character of Baldwins. Aumonier has also raised, and perhaps, with the story, answered, the question of what we want to do with our 'littery society'. The 'intellectual standard' is raised by Alf's striving to articulate his experience in the desert – which I'll save to the end - but not by Baldwin's glib articulation of 'tortuous metaphysics'.

Alf's journey leads to Annie returning her engagement ring, with the comment that ' a book lowse is worse than no good,' but this leads to a tearful meeting between the two that is witnessed by Weeks. When Alf resigns from the society, Weeks does not sever their connection, but develops it further. He sends Alf fifty pounds - a considerable amount in those days - to help furnish his new marital home, and encourages him to continue to borrow books:

> 'I was to go on readin the books he says I shall find good things in them...'

It is a thoughtful story, but its main achievement from a writing perspective – the 'how', rather than the 'about,' is in solving of that problem of how to express a profound experience within the straightjacket of a limited vocabulary, and using poor articulation, all without reducing the speaker – or letter writer – to a pastiche or caricature of himself. What Alf and Annie and Weeks and all the others write to each other, is what Aumonier is writing to us. It is what Weeks has recognised when he observes Annie and Alf's tearful re-union. Aumonier, I suspect, is one of those writers who recognises that it is worthwhile to remind us that we are, and can be, better than we think we are, which might account for how well he was loved as an individual, if what few accounts of him that I have found are to be believed.

'You think of the other fellow over there whose thinkin like you are perhaps and he all alone to lookin up the blinkin stars and it comes over you that its only love that holds us all together love and nothing else at all.'

2 DID YOU SEE HIM? 'THE SEAL' BY L.A.G.STRONG

In his brief biographical note on L.A.G.Strong, Philip Hensher, in *The Penguin Book of the British Short Story*, says, 'The near total decline of his reputation after his death is something of a puzzle, given his writing's consistent quality and penetration.'

Of the thirty or so Strong stories that I have read – all in *Travellers*, a Readers Union/Methuen 1947 collection - a handful particularly appeal. *The Rook*, which Hensher included in his anthology, is one, and *The White Cottage*, which I have written about elsewhere, is another. A third is *The Seal*.

In a story about a sea creature that appears from and disappears into the depths, it is probably no surprise that I looked for, and found, something deeper in the story than the events it described. It's a simple story. Rosamund, holidaying with the boisterous George, a year after their honeymoon, takes a walk to the beach, where she sees a seal to which she sings. Boisterously, George joins her, driving the seal away.

There's more to it than that, of course. It is a story about surfaces, and what we do, or do not see beneath them. The seeing is mostly done by Rosamund, and perhaps by us, and the not seeing, by George, and hopefully not us!

Strong, along with many who write, I suspect, likes to hide a secret or two in his stories. One in *The Seal* might be the location of the beach, for in this story a reference to a dog called Darach reminds me that there is a beach (since featured in the film *Local Hero*) called Camus Darrach – Darrach being the Scots Gaelic word for Oak (Scots Gaelic being an English term for the Scots Gaelic word 'Ghallic') – that in many particulars is just like the beach Rosamund visits. Though that might be co-incidental.

It could be co-incidental too that the verb Strong uses for George's dash to the beach, which drives away the seal, is 'to plunge.' 'He plunged up, panting, to where she sat.' More obvious than the connections between George and the seal, are the disconnections between him and Rosamund.

These disconnections are quietly placed, but explicit, and they begin at the first sentence.

> 'Just before six the rain lifted at last, and Rosamund started off to the shore by herself.'

There's economy here. That 'at last' adds disproportionately more to our understanding of the situation than its two words might suggest. But 'by herself' is the more potent addition, bringing nothing to the description except to specify her aloneness. The next sentence begins with 'George,' a powerful juxtaposition in itself, but the later phrases, 'given up hope' and 'loud in his outbursts' begin a process of filling in our sense of Rosamund's husband. George has put off writing letters, obstinately: 'he would not begin,' 'pacing up and down' and, perhaps more tellingly, 'Characteristically, he would not...'

What Rosamund is doing closes the paragraph, 'going down to the shore to wait for him.' If any story carries layers of meaning, this one does. We learn more about George but, perhaps because we are told what he is, rather than, as with Rosamund, what she does, we know that it is she who will be our main focus. George is 'a large fretful man.'

Thwarted in his desires he would spend 'the evening trying not to have a grievance; a generous effort, so patent, and so unsuccessful.' At first I thought that 'patent' a typo for 'patient,' but of course the more unusual word is just the right one.

Rosamund's walk gives us the chance to see her more clearly. We learn that she has a sense of belonging to this place: 'She had spent every summer here since she could remember.' Having George along, though, has changed the experience, and the difference between what they experience is emphasised. 'There had been a great deal more for her' than the 'immediate beauties' that George boisterously reacts to. George's personality, we are told, 'was so loud...'

A neat comparison between the two is in the way he will pick up and sing, 'in a loud baritone, the tune she was quietly whistling...' Strong, perhaps to make sure we do get it, gives us the first of a pair of contrasting images, the second of which will appear towards the end: Rosamund 'did not like breaking the pure snowy face of the sandhills with great sliding footsteps,' and so she by-passes them. When George arrives, near the end of the story, he will come 'charging headlong......bringing down avalanches with each leap.'

The story, about clumsiness and sensitivity, and about what is lost in the meeting of the two, draws power from Strong's description of Rosamund's wooing of the seal, in comparison to George's driving it away.

'Oh,' breathed Rosamund, heart-broken, 'don't go away.' This is before George has arrived, when the seal has first seen her; but she wins it back, by whistling to it. 'She put into the notes her soul.' In an extended passage, the seal is seduced to re-surface, and come closer. 'slowly and softly the big seal swam towards her,' and at that 'big,' I thought of George.

    'Oh, bless you,' she breathed, 'bless you, you darling.'

    Then she sings, and the seal listens 'with soft eyes, in attention and vague delight.' It is a seduction and 'It should have lasted for ever.'

But George's 'hearty voice' arrives, as he devastates those dunes. The seal regards him for a while, and then 'without reproach,' dives out of sight. George has caught a glimpse, and responds in his usual way, 'bellowed excitedly,' Strong says.

There then follows a remarkable statement, that shows the glimmer, and limitations also of George's awareness, and which also brings together the different levels of meaning in this rich story: 'I'd no idea they came in so close.' He ends by asking Rosamund if she has seen, and her bleak reply closes the story: 'Yes,' said Rosamund.'

I've mentioned the parallels I find between George and the seal. Are they me 'flooding wretched material' with my own ideas, as C.S.Lewis warned against? I think not. There is a moment when Rosamund stops singing, and the seal 'blew and made a commotion in the water, till she began again.' That seems very George-like to me.

I find this a powerful and very human tale of lost potential, of a closeness of which George had 'no idea' but which Rosamund saw, and which 'should have lasted forever.' It is, quite simply, a love story.

3 BREAKING THE MOULD
A TURNING POINT IN ELIZABETH BOWEN'S
COLLECTED SHORT STORIES

Reading from beginning to end of Elizabeth Bowen's chronologically laid out Collected short stories, I reached The War Years. The bulk of the collection was behind me now, written during the twenties and thirties. The last two sections combined are smaller than The Thirties, and I'm struck by a sense of her trajectory being on a downward curve. That isn't to say that the individual stories are not strong, but that the sense of an ending coming is so much stronger.

The second story in The War Years section is a departure though, an experiment in storytelling that appears nowhere in any of the preceding sections. *Oh, Madam...* is a true wartime story, far more than the preceding *Unwelcome Idea*, set in an oddly British, rather than foreign and neutral, Dublin. It's not the time and place that make *Oh, Madam...* so innovative in Bowen's work. It is the choice of narrative voice, and perspective. This story is in effect a monologue. Not merely a first person narrative, it is one half of a dialogue spoken between a housemaid and her returning mistress.

'Oh, madam........Oh, *madam*, here you are!'

Even the opening is radically different from previous stories, for the title is echoed twice in the first four words. I can't remember seeing another story in this collection, or indeed any other, where this technique is used. To reference a title tends to 'use it up' rather than emphasise it. It is often a revelation to reach the reference that will throw the title into sharp meaning, but here is a repetition that we must be reluctant to categorise as 'mere'. It's worth noting too, that the title includes those three dots that will come to signal unspoken interjection of the mistress' words, and their implied meanings.

The house has been blitzed, and Bowen, in the maid's, not the mistress' voice, speaks. Sometimes there are no dots, and only from responses to them do we guess, perhaps with less certainty than people who lived through the blitz would have guessed, what has been said.

'I don't know what you'll say. Look, sit down just for a minute,Madam; I dusted this chair for you. Yes, the hall's all right really; You don't see so much at first-only, our beautiful fanlight gone.'

The subtle introduction to what has happened is remarkable. Only at that fanlight do we get an inkling, which makes us revise our understanding of what we have previously been told, about why, for example, the chair needs dusting. Bowen winds us in to a fuller understanding of what has taken place, exactly as madam is wound in, with the words of her maid. Even that comma, after 'only', signals the hesitation that comes before the revelation.

There is nothing remotely like this in any of the earlier stories: not the perspective, not the voice, and of course, not in the subject matter. In a Bowen short story context, this is a shot in the dark, an experiment in form, and a response to entirely new circumstances in the world around her. If short stories truly are about situation, as Florence Goyet suggests, then here is an actual situation unfolding before the writer. If the earlier stories are reflections upon what are, and have been the norms of Bowen's life - her class perspectives - here is a story about what is happening now, a response rather than a reflection. In that sense it is a journalistic, as much as a literary story.

Yet the detail of the content, as opposed to its location and ambience, is still the same. Bowen is looking at the minutiae of daily life in the sort of middle class household that employed staff, and travelled extensively, and had connections that would allow them to move to the country to live with 'her ladyship,' as the unvoiced mistress does here. She is also examining the relationship between the two women, and the relationship between them and the house that has been blasted.

> 'Oh, *I'm* quite all right, madam. I made some tea this morning......Do I? Oh well, that's natural, I suppose.'

The unreported comment is implied by the question that follows it, but Bowen becomes more overt as the maid talks about other houses that have been hit.

> 'Little houses aren't strong, madam.'

She is talking of her sister's house, and of the poorer houses throughout the city. Yet what is more striking, is Bowen's presentation of their differing attitudes to what they must do next.

> '*But you couldn't ever, not this beautiful house!* You couldn't ever....I know many ladies *are*.'

The thought precedes the outburst, but her lady is abandoning the house. It is the maid, who has already offered, referring to the fallen plaster, to 'have it all off in a day or two.' Her lady is made of less stern stuff though, and after the discussion of what needs to be removed, it is the maid who offers to stay to whatever bitter end will follow: 'That really is what I'd rather, if you have no objection.' This is the strongest indictment so far in the collection, I feel, that Bowen has levelled against her class, and though we perceive it through the maid's words, it is not an indictment brought by the maid herself. Perhaps because neither is named, they become representative, rather than being characters, and we must ask if the maid's voice is stereotypical, or a caricature. Angus Wilson, in his introduction, cites it as an example of the 'fault' in Bowen's ear:

'...on the level of the H.M.Tennent matinee performance that it became.'

I'm not familiar with that, but, if he's suggesting the maid's voice is lacking credibility, then perhaps there's a fault with my ear too. Perhaps the passage of time has blunted both the voice and the hearing, but however accurate, or stereotypical the voice may be, it is what the maid has to say that makes this story worth our attention as writers; not necessarily because of its meaning, but because of its method of approaching the content.

What the house, and the life within it, has been is obliquely probed, as well as what it has become. Coming to a story like this, at this moment in a collection, and perceiving it to be so different makes it like a mirror, for mirrors show what stands behind us. The stories that stand behind, that went before this one, seem homogenous in their differences. But if we go on beyond *Oh, Madam...*, we get to *Summer Night*, and it is as if the mould has been broken, for here again, Bowen is trying a form that we have not seen before anywhere in the collection.

Is it that the war, destroying much, has enabled her to break free of the writer she has been? Is that trajectory I began with still, in fact, on the rising curve?

The change that occurs with *Oh Madam...* is not a short term one. The story seems to signal the arrival of new sort of story within the collection, yet Elizabeth Bowen doesn't repeat the innovation of this story. There are no more monologue voices, nor any development of the maid's voice that tells it, but neither is there a return to the style of story that had gone before. It's as if Bowen, from this point on, was re-discovering her genre.

Of course this might be a quirk of the compiler's imagination, as much as of the writer's development, but it is what we are presented with in *The Collected Short Stories* and we're entitled to react to it as such.

In *Summer Night*, we get another, quite different innovation. Here Bowen experiments with multiple narrators. The story is passed from one to the other, but not simply that. Rather, it is that each narrator has a different story to tell in the overarching sequence of imagined events that take place over the eponymous time-span. This is not the more conventional changing viewpoint of a single sequence of events, but a series of what are almost entirely different stories that coincide rather than interlink over the course of an evening. One effect of this is to blur the focus of the story. Which character does the story really belong to? The answer of course, is to no single one of them, but to all. Here we have a series of separate stories that happen together.

The stories that follow *Oh Madam...* seem more obscure. The detail within them is as precise and clear as that given in earlier stories, but its significance is harder to judge. Is this how authors develop? Do they raise their game, and expect us to raise ours? Or do they go more deeply – probably the most succinct and best piece of advice I was given, by Tom Pow, as a writer during the whole two years of my M.Litt course at Glasgow University – into their own perspectives, and leave us behind?

In the context of poetry I have heard writers say, and have read, that it is best to forget meaning, and just enjoy the experience, but I've never been entirely convinced. I've enjoyed songs sung in a language that I don't speak, and I've sensed the emotion that they seem to evoke, but when I read or listen to *Jabberwocky* being read, I instinctively try to make sense of it. I attribute meanings, and images to its words. I know what my 'slithy toves' look like.

Perhaps because of this pre-disposition, as a reader, I find the later stories in Bowen's collection, harder to understand, and thus dissatisfying. Story as puzzle is not the same as subtle story. I want that 'flash of wings' that C.S.Lewis tells us is the best a writer can hope to give the reader of what is caught briefly in the net of story.

I wonder if this is touching on a fundamental difference between two contending modes of storytelling. Is there an older tradition, in which the storyteller tried to share something they had perceived, and a more modern one in which the attempt is to communicate what has been experienced, and to leave the perceptions to the reader, or listener? Perhaps the two are not modern and ancient at all, but have co-existed since the very first story, but like finely balanced scales, dipping between one and the other at different times. Has Bowen, as this collection turns towards its final pieces, moved between those two types?

Story works by a process of continuous contextualisation and re-contextualisation. Each word, potentially, creates the context in which we shall apprehend the next, and re-creates the context in which all the words that have passed must be seen. The changes may be incremental or catastrophic. They might deepen, or subvert the existing context. Is the same true, I wonder, for the sequenced stories in a printed collection? If authors and publishers spend time ordering the stories in a collection, they must do so with the intention of creating an effect that can only be experienced if the collection is read in the order it is printed. Casual conversation, and my own practice, suggests that this is unlikely to happen, yet it must be true to some extent, that the stories we have just read, even if from another collection, and by another author, must form the context in which we read the next.

For Bowen's collection, and for any other we tackle, is it worth reading in order to get that collective contextualisation, assuming it was created deliberately, or should we treat the stories within as individuals in their own right? The sequence of printing does not assure, though it might imply, a sequence of writing. It does not even mean there was a similar sequence of publishing in magazines and journals, yet the presentation of the collected stories in a specifically time-ordered format, as this one is, invites us to look for a trajectory within it.

I have read the 'collected' works of several short story writers, and the entire published works (so far as I know) of one or two. In all cases, one or two stories, sometimes several, have stood out from the mass. I've found a similar phenomenon in poetry. A favourite poet, or short story writer, might have published hundreds of works, yet one or two, at most a handful, however many one enjoys, will stand out as being particularly resonant with your own insights and perceptions of life. Whether or not it is these, or something more communal that makes a writer 'great', or even if such terms are useful, is another discussion. But in the case of the Bowen collection, the ordering of the stories, and the reading of them in that order, has raised for me the issue of whether or not the particular prominence of *Oh Madam...*to my reading, has been a result of its intrinsic qualities, or of its positioning within the larger group.

4 ILLUMINATING THE GHOSTS STORIES OF M.R.JAMES (1862-1936)

Reading the *Collected Ghost Stories* of M.R.James, the counties of Suffolk, Norfolk and Cambridgeshire, rural even today, loom large. As the Snows (pere et fils) showed in a TV examination of who owns Britain, lift off in a helicopter and even now, you will find that behind the crust of buildings that lines our roads, there lurks an atavistic, and largely deserted countryside.

A friend of mine, several years ago, was surprised when a visiting African commented, why you live so close to the river, man? Rivers in Africa are not so benign as ours, until recently, have seemed to be. Had he asked the same of the woods, my friend would possibly not have been so taken aback, but then my friend did not live close to the woods! Woods, along with sea-shores and flat lands, and farmers' fields are the places in which the past in all its atavistic gory, in barrows and graveyards, and gloomy tangled ruins is only waiting for their ghostly stories to be stumbled upon. And unless we live in the major conurbations, and perhaps, even there, they are only a few paces down the lane or round the corner.

These are the settings for M.R.James' haunting stories, where our view is restricted by trees or tangled undergrowth, by sea mist; where unknown threats wait, where escape is hampered by thorns or, as in *A*

Warning to the Curious by soft shingle and groynes. His stories are built on what is just out of sight, or not seen clearly, or not there when we look again. Often they are stories passed on by somebody to whom they have been told, or who was a witness to them rather than the one to whom they happened. Malevolence and retribution often drive them, with death the reward for interference in what was better left undisturbed.

Trying to isolate what it is I like about them raises questions of form and content, and especially of narrative voice, for what binds these stories is not simply similarity of subject or ghostliness, but a sense of the way the stories are being, and might well have been, told.

His narrators are always male, middle class, and of a certain age. They speak with confidence, in their stories, in themselves. They do not fear the ridicule of their listeners, though they sometimes doubt they will be believed. They know they will be listened to.

The content nearly always involves antiquarian concerns: ruins, artefacts, memories – the mythical memories of an England that stretches back to Roman times and beyond, precedes, in fact, English. All these elements are in what is probably his best known story, and perhaps the most typical. Set on the East Anglian coast it concerns a young professor who takes an ancient whistle from an archaeological site, and blows it! He raises a violent and unnatural wind, which leads on to some odd events. A fellow guest at the hotel where he is staying warns him to throw away the whistle – Colonel Wilson has been in India, and has thus seen such marvels before! But the professor does not believe in such irrationalities, and suffers the consequences. He is attacked in his room by an evil spirit. The good Colonel comes to the rescue, the whistle is cast out to sea, and the professor returns home with his beliefs shaken. The story is, of course, *Oh, Whistle, And I'll Come To You, My Lad*. It's a story in which not much has really happened, certainly no death, such as closes several other stories, but the bones of a James' story are there.

And the ending, almost benign, tentative rather than decisive, what is that doing? Could it be that shaking the professor's dis-belief is a way of shaking ours, and making us more credulous for the next story? Could it be that not having a 'horrible' ending, James is making sure we're not put off from the next one?

Certainly, there are endings in which the protagonist dies, but those deaths – as in *Casting The Runes* – do not overtake the narrator! Another feature of the stories is the way those narrators engage with the reader. We are always conscious that we are being told a story. We are not witnessing one unfold, but hearing about how one had unfolded. If James is raising fears in us, he is also allaying them by these distancing techniques. He is always reminding us of the presence of the teller.

Conversational asides, such as 'I dare say you know it' when a town is named, and 'a person who is not in the story' to describe a speaker who is merely setting up the situation bring the narrator into focus. Elsewhere a footnote corrects a fact misreported by one of the characters, and sometimes the narrator will quite disclaim knowledge of details. In fact, in one place he actually suggests the reader supply 'appropriate digressions' on a subject of which he knows nothing! In what we might call descriptive lists he peters out with 'etc' and 'and so forth.' Details, he is telling us, are all well and good, but you can make up your own. It's the gist that he's really interested in, and so should you be! All these narratorial intrusions reinforce our sense of a story being told, person to person, and perhaps man to man. For James' narrators are all men, and perhaps his audiences, especially those he directly told the stories to, were also male.

Women do not feature greatly in any of these ghostly tales. There are maids and servants and housekeepers, and wives, but they are never the protagonists. The stories always happen to men, often boyish ones, and always from the gentlemanly class – meaning those who do not work with their hands. Even in *The Haunted Dolls House* the story is about the two men who have bought and sold it. In the story *The*

Residence at Whitminster the niece, Mary has a prominent role, but it is her uncle and her fiancée, along with two past boy victims who dominate the story. Yet James is not so much writing about the men as about the situations they become caught in, and they are men like he was, whose lives are centred on the cloister and the study, the library and the out-of-town hotel; lives that are lived within stone walls and dark wood panelled rooms where evening sunlight slants through tall windows casting an orange glow over those who listen to their stories.

In his Preface James discounts his own skills as a writer but in the final piece, *Stories I Have Tried To Write* he gives some brief glimpses of himself at work. These can give encouragement to the practising writer, even if he or she is not engaged with the same genre, for he tells us the bones of stories that he could not flesh out, and gives us the faces of stories for which he could provide no skeletal structure. It was in this self deprecatory piece that I found a rare example of James' humour:

'Be careful how you handle the packet you pick up on the carriage -drive, particularly if it contains nail parings and hair. Do not in any case bring it into the house. It may not be alone… (Dots are believed by many writers of our day to be a good substitute for effective writing).'

Ouch!...

5 THE MORAL CROSSROADS OF MARC LE GOUPILS

I know nothing of Marc Le Goupils, save for one line of commentary in the introductory essay to the volume in which I found his story, *The Cross-Roads*, translated from the French by an undisclosed translator.

That one line tells me that Marc increased the strength of the neo-realistic movement in the French short story, combining elements of several other national strains. His story, it says, is bitter. Indeed it is. *The Cross-Roads* is bitter almost, but not quite, to the point of comedy. Indeed, the danger for the writer with such stories must be that they might be laughed at, rather than cried over.

The eponymous crossroads is at the precise point where four parishes meet, and here arrives, from who knows where, one night, a dying woman. 'An unknown woman. Age supposed about sixty.' There is speculation about her origins, and her type: 'not even one of those ordinary beggars…..She was a gypsy, an inveterate wanderer, living on the road by petty thefts.'

What intrigues me about many of the French short story writers I have encountered, from the twentieth, nineteenth, eighteenth centuries and even earlier, is that they seem to possess a lightness of touch, even in telling the grimmest of tales. Le Goupils story begins with the discovery of the dead woman, from which in flash-back it goes on to detail the miserable hours of her dying.

> 'The only important point was that her death was due to natural causes.'

Towards the end of the beginning, this apparently clear statement opens the canette-de-vers that is the rest of the story.

> 'The death of this poor woman had, indeed, been the most natural in the world, and no fewer than fifteen witnesses, were ready to testify to this.'

This repetition, a few lines on gives us some key words, even in translation, for it is what we mean by 'natural' that we are about to witness. Like the cameo part in a block-buster movie, our dying gypsy doesn't get much of a role. She has no lines to speak, only a few moans and groans, sighs and wheezes, as she noisily expires. We do not learn her name, but we know well enough what she symbolises, and, in that sense, who she is.

The story is not really about her. It is about the good people of the parishes upon whose mercy she has been cast in her final hours. And they are good people. They take her in, to begin with.

Principal among them is the Blacksmith of Carrefour-de-la-Forge (Crossroads of the Forge) and his wife, Mistress Nails. Nails, unlike Carrrefour, has been translated into English, there being, according to my Dictionnaire Nouveau – of an age closer to that of the writer than to my own – no French words 'nails'. This suggests that the name is not randomly chosen, and this story does confront our Blacksmith and his hard-as wife with several choices. These two, more than any other characters in the story, are at that 'moral' crossroads.

There's a subtlety to the presentation of the statement the Blacksmith poses to the begger, when he goes to her assistance, to begin with : 'Hello, mother, you don't seem quite as well as you might be!' He says it in 'a voice which sounded kindly'.

This is a story about seeming kindly, to begin with. Mistress Nails soon hits it on the head: 'She's a deader, I do believe.' Le Goupils tells us: 'They were good people, and very neighbourly,' and this is a story about goodness, and neighbourliness, to begin with.

Country people though, he reminds us, are often 'by no means well off' and these two do 'not consider that they had any duty to fulfil to strangers and tramps.' Yet, when the old woman gasps and begins to totter, the Blacksmith's wife rushes to catch her, and they agree, instinctively, that they must help her. She is taken into their house, and placed upon a chair. The Blacksmith first becomes uneasy: 'Can't you see that she is dying?' and wants to 'cure' her: 'so that she can go away soon'.

It is not that they don't want to help. They give her brandy, a consciously generous slug of it. The neighbours arrive to see what is going on, and 'each inwardly thanked his lucky stars' that the duty of care has fallen on the Blacksmith, whom they 'praised highly.' For a while, it looks as if they can get her well enough to go back outside. The night will be balmy enough not to kill her! The Blacksmith wants to be reassured of his duty, but the neighbours slope off, one by one, leaving him to struggle with his conscience alone. The wife sends him for a priest, or a doctor, saying they will keep her till tomorrow.

Outside though, one of the neighbours has heard that 'if that woman dies in your house Blosseville (*the parish*) will have to pay the funeral expenses.' Fear of the Mayor, the magistrate, and the police, of the red tape and regulations, and expense, from now on dominates the Blacksmith's thinking. His wife is convinced immediately of the wisdom of his resolve:

'I can't have her any longer,' he declared'

'One can't do these things all alone' she said...' and then:

'Fetch Gaffer Durand's wheelbarrow...'

'Dur' is the French word for 'hard', 'durant' for enduring. Durand might have translated as Gaffer Harding. Just a thought!

Then begin the darkly comic events that fill the latter half of the story, as, laid, almost reverently, with a soft pillow to support her head, in the wheelbarrow, she is trundled from place to place in search of somewhere she can die, at someone else's expense. Even this proves not so simple to the good folk of the parishes, for as each location is attempted, it is thwarted by the wishes of other good people.

The nearer she comes to death, the more urgently they seek to dump her. She is lifted gently from the barrow, and placed back in it more roughly. The pillow is retrieved: she will not need it much longer. As her gasps and cries become weaker, the search becomes more frenetic. Eventually, in the dead of night, she is tipped out unceremoniously, and the wheelbarrow clatters back as unburdened as those who wheel it.

Marc Le Goupils' realism keeps the telling of these quasi-farcial events just on the right side of serious. We never laugh at her, the dying woman, whose groans and whimpers are heard often enough to remind us she is there, and living, but whose silences are long enough for us almost to forget. Out of the realism, and the faux-comedy, is borne the realisation of the moral vacuum in which these shallowly caring people live – wishing to ease her passing, and to show their humanity, but not at the cost of their own labours, and their own pockets. The value of the living and the dead is also weighed. In so much as she lives, she demands their sympathy, but the nearer to death they perceive her to be, the further she slips below the horizon of their care.

Structurally it is split, by 'white space' breaks into eight segments. The first sets the scene: the fact of the body. The second flashes back to the Blacksmith and his wife finding her, alive, and taking her in. The third deals with the neighbours' input. The fourth, quite short, has Gaffer Durand checking the weather. The fifth recounts his discussions with the Blacksmith, leading to that wheelbarrow. The sixth and seventh tell the blackly comic story of the quest to find a place to dump the dying woman, and the final one, briefly, closes the account: 'the Brettevillians and the Blossevillians went to bed and slept soundly.'

It is such a grim story, but so finely handled. The reader does not burst out laughing, though laughter bubbles. The story is not unremittingly unsympathetic. We feel, almost, sorry for the villagers, as they struggle to square the petty selfishness of their actions with the seriousness of the dying woman's plight.

And, of course, at heart, such stories as this, whenever they were, or are, or shall be written, call out to the petty selfishness in us. How shall we behave in similar circumstances, beneath the shadow of our own petty regulations and limitations; when we reach our moral crossroads?

[You can find The Cross Roads in Volume 6 of Hammerton's The World's Thousand Best Short Stories, c1933. It is one of a dozen and more stories by 'later' French writers who are represented by only one story each in the collection.]

6 HALLMARKING THE STORIES OF PROSPER MERIMEE

I hadn't encountered Prosper Mérimée (1803–1870) before reading a handful of his stories in *The World's Thousand Best Short Stories*, published in 1933. Opera buffs might know him as the originator of the story *Carmen*. Others may have seen his stories in *The Twelve Best Short Stories in the French Language* from 1920, or the Folio Society's 1998 *Book of French Short Stories*. The editor of the latter, Brian Masters, gives us some brief comments on Mérimée's work:

> [He] strove to ensure that his work was terse, clear, vivid and concise, shorn of verbosity. He was a master at shining light on a significant detail which he sought to illuminate, and one suspects the detail was the grain from which the story grew.

If this paints Mérimée as someone with whom those of us striving to write today can identify, then what Edward Wright (who provides the introduction to Volume III of the *The World's Thousand Best Short Stories*) says will seem more of a point: 'Mérimée is the creator of the modern *conte*.'

Conte, if you're not of the academic persuasion, turns out to be the French word for 'story'. ***The Penguin Dictionary of Literary Terms*** gives 'tales, story', and points out that Guy de Maupassant referred to his short stories as *contes*. Brian Masters gives us a quotation from Mérimée: 'Je n'aime dans l'histoire que les anecdotes.' Cast into good northern English, this would be something like: 'I like nowt but anecdotes (lad).'***The Penguin Dictionary*** also points out that the conte should be 'a little fantastic', which it then refines in parentheses to 'not realistic', before adding 'droll and witty'. In practice, the accuracy of this, I suspect, hangs on the word 'little' and the reminder that reality often can be stranger than fiction.

Mérimée's seven stories that are collected in **The World's Thousand Best Short Stories**, at first, seemed a disparate grouping. I wondered, is there a Prosper Mérimée stamp upon them? Is there the common hallmark of the short story, whatever that might be?

In 'Mateo Falcone', as Professor Charles E. May points out in the opening chapter of *The Short Story: The Reality of Artifice*, Mérimée takes a folktale-like story, but makes it grimly real. Set in Corsica, it recounts a short series of events, in which the eponymous father kills his clever, but covetous, ten-year-old son for betraying a fugitive to his pursuers. The story has an interesting and distinct structure, for it falls into two parts, each itself divided. Firstly, the scene is set, in landscape and in society. Notably, we learn of the Maquis, a shrub-land where fugitives are safe by virtue of its close growth and abundant food on the hoof (and the support of local shepherds): 'The *maquis* is the home of the Corsican peasant and of whoever is in trouble with the police.'

It is a creation of lazy farmers, who burn off the top-growth of trees to make a fertile ash in which to grow their crops, leaving the roots to sprout ever more thickly afterwards. Both real, and metaphorical, this landscape enables and mirrors what is happening in the human story.

While his mother and father (Mateo) are away hunting in the Maquis, Fortunato encounters the fugitive, out of whom he negotiates five francs for hiding him. Moments later he equally boldly negotiates a pocket watch out of the pursuing soldiers, for betraying where he has hidden the bandit. First, the fugitive is outfaced by Fortunato:

> "Come, hide me, or I'll kill you."
> "Your gun is not loaded, and there are no cartridges in your bandolier."

> Next, the adjutant gets equally short shrift:

> "...haven't you seen a man go by?"
> "Have I seen a man go by?"
> "Yes; a man with a pointed cap and a waistcoat worked in red and yellow."
> "A man with a pointed cap and a waistcoat worked in red and yellow?"

Then Mateo and his wife return. In contrast to the insolent, precocious bantering of Fortunato comes a far more tense and threatening tone between Mateo and the leader of the soldiers. The soldier reveals what Fortunato has done and, after the soldier has gone, Mateo leads the boy off into the wilderness. Implacable in his determination, Mateo resists his son's pleas, makes him say his prayers, and then shoots him. The story is brutal, short and uncompromising, as is its setting.

If this is the beginning of the modern conte, then is it also a benchmark for the other stories of Mérimée? 'The Etruscan Vase' seems quite different, telling of a love affair troubled by the jealousy of the main protagonist. The character Saint-Clair is a nineteenth century equivalent of a stereotypical 'lad'. Well heeled, and one of a louche group of male friends who rib each other and indulge in what we would now think of as sexist banter, Saint-Clair's feelings are focussed on the eponymous crock, given to the lady in the piece by a previous lover. Or so he thinks. Her apparent love for the vase, he believes, reflects her love for the other man. Irked by his feelings, Saint-Clair reacts angrily to the taunts of the friend who has told him about the lover in the first place, and a dual is proposed. Then Saint-Clair, confronting the woman, discovers that the other man had not been taken seriously and is, in fact, considered a joke. She reads out a love letter from Massigny 'amid bursts of laughter!'

Suddenly, Saint-Clair sees his error.

"I am a wretch… They told me you had loved Massigny, and–"
"Massigny!" and she began to laugh.

The vase is smashed to prove it. Saint-Clair is overjoyed and plans to apologise to his friend, but first, gallantly, he will let him have the first shot. Of course, the first shot turns out to be fatal and the two stories, despite their widely different settings and tones, come to a similar, brutal end.

Looking more closely we see again that use of the setting: the physical and the social, enabling and creating the possibility of the story taking place. The actual ending is not the shooting of Saint-Clair, but a discussion about it, and the recounting of the dual, by two of the other 'lads'. After that, a further paragraph tells what has happened to the Countess, who has pined to death for loss of her lover.

These two stories have that heightened sense of tragedy that Romance demands. Not only is the loss irrevocable but also it is entirely unnecessary, except by the choices that the people, in those places, at those times, in the physical and social settings in which they existed, felt that they had to make.

'Tamango' is a much more difficult story for a twenty-first century reader to tackle, for it deals with the slave trade, and not explicitly in condemnation of it. Briefly, Tamango is a native slaver, who is captured along with the slaves he is selling, but who leads a rebellion on board ship. The crew is slaughtered, but the ship is beyond the technical knowledge of the freed slaves. They drift and die, finding the on-board alcohol, debauching and fighting while the unmanned ship disintegrates around them. Finally, only Tamango is left to be rescued by a British frigate. Taken to the West Indies, he recovers his health and, because he has only acted in self-defence (and killed only Frenchmen, not British), he is given a sinecure of six sous a day, plus food. Eventually, he becomes the cymbal-player of a regimental band. But he drinks 'rum and grog in inordinate quantities, and dies 'in hospital of inflammation of the lungs'. Again, setting, combined with social mores, creates the story, and for three out of three, we end with death.

Two more of the stories go the same way. In 'The Game of Backgammon' a penitent gambler, who believes he has lost his reputation by cheating at Backgammon, persuades a shipmate to kill him, if battle does not! But the story is a framed story, being told to a passenger by the captain of a whaler, and at the moment when the friend must perform his duty, a whale is spotted and the captain breaks off his narrative. We are left to speculate, not *if* the protagonist dies, but *how*, which, of course, raises the sort of speculation we have been confronted with before. Again, it is a function of physical and social setting. In 'The Taking of the Redoubt' the same is true. A colonel's last words confirm the soldierly bombast that a young subaltern, pushed up through the ranks as his superiors are killed, has struggled to find in himself.

'The Venus of Ille' has a death too, that of the old man who invites the narrator to his rural village to see the eponymous statue. It is an ancient bronze and seems to have a malevolent power: a worker is crushed by it; a boy throwing stones is hit by the ricochet; more frighteningly, the new son-in-law of the old man, on his wedding night, is killed by the statue, and the daughter driven insane by seeing the crime. Nobody, of course believes her, but we do. The narrator is telling of long past events, including the death of the old man, which follows a few years after, but he ends his story with a P.S. The statue has been melted down, and cast into bells for the local church: 'Since this bell began to ring at Ille the vines have twice been frosted.' Look at the syntax of that closing sentence – 'frosted twice' would be a much more natural expression, but the meaning of the sentence and the true end to the story have been manipulated into the very last word, 'frosted'. The split infinitive has earned its keep.

This story can be found in **The Twelve Best Short Stories in the French Language** anthology. Written, or at least first published in 1837, this placing in the 'Twelve Best' makes a very serious claim for for the story, especially in 1920 when there is almost another hundred years to pick from. Of the seven stories I have looked at, it is, in several respects, the best. It has the element of outright magic, which the others do not, and, in having that magic, it has broken the recurrent train of setting, up to a point.

The narrator here is a Parisian, his host a countryman, though 'a very learned antiquary'. Much is made of that difference, mostly by M. Puygarrig, the host. By placing the visit on the days of a country wedding, where the social backwardness of the country folk can be revealed, Mérimée has increased our awareness of the difference. There is, too, a party of Aragonese shepherds present, against whom the son-in-law to be plays tennis, and one of whom he insults. They are country people as well and atavistic in some degree. The wedding allows highlights of this divide, providing discussion of ring giving habits – contrasting the Parisian sophistication of the simple band with rural ostentation.

The wedding ring gets placed on the finger of the statue during the tennis game and cannot be removed for the ceremony. This is a further development of the malevolence attributed to the statue, yet still within the bounds of possibility. That final murder, though, is quite out of bounds, but, then again, it is only recounted by the maddened, widowed daughter. The Parisian narrator, by confessing his almost belief, encourages ours. He can find no other explanation. So setting and belief are again crucial to the story, linking it once more with the others.

Which leaves 'The Blue Room'. If I tell you that this story ends with the sentence 'Prepare a really good lunch for us at twelve', you might expect a lighter tone and a happier story, and you would be right to do so. A couple fleeing from their situations stay a night in a hotel, under assumed names. They endure the noisy, rude banter of some soldiers in another room and encounter an Englishman with a seemingly unsavoury cousin. Eventually, they get what they have come for: the tranquility and passion of each other's company. But when the man wakes in the night he hears a bump next door, where the Englishman sleeps, and thinks he hears soft footsteps retreating. He sees a dark, red liquid oozing under the rooms' connecting door.

Murder has obviously been done and the couple are witnesses, perhaps even suspects! They are there under a false name, after all. They must flee and are preparing to do so when – as the eagle eyed reader might have guessed, for there is a clue – the truth is revealed: there has been no murder and there will be no enquiry, nor pursuit, which leads to that last line about lunch.

And here, in this light and humorous piece, which typifies for me a style of French stories that I found in Bonaventure des Périers' fourteenth century 'The Cobbler Blondeau', we have the same necessity of setting, physical and social, to enable and create the events. Once again we are led towards death, and death by murder, and the trapping of the innocent in a snare they have laid for themselves. But here it is all a trick, a trick played on us by the author, unless we have caught his sleight of hand.

In Florence Goyet's *The Classic Short Story*, much is made of the short story being about situation rather than character. Though they come from a time before the period this book examines, I think all of these stories fully endorse that view. It is a hallmark of the genre.

7 'THE LIBRARY WINDOW' BY MARGARET OLIPHANT

Margaret Oliphant was a popular and successful Victorian novelist.

An Irish writer once compared the short story form, or at least our interest in it, with a horse race. *The Library Window* offers something more like a snail race, at least for the first 25 pages. Telling detail gives way to tedious re-told detail, as the eponymous window is described, and described, and minutely described, over and over again. It is an incrementally added to description being built up in the mind of the young girl whose story this really is, as she sits and watches a window across the street from her Aunt Mary's house.

It is a window that will bear watching, for Aunt Mary's visitors cannot even be sure that it is actually a window! It might be purely ornamental, a painted stone, or a blocked window. Aunt Mary knows, we sense, but she's not letting on. The young girl though, sees it in increasing detail, and the room behind it. The story hints that it might be one of those Victorian ghost stories. It is a Scottish story, and the Scots, we know, can be fey.

The long slow build up does lead to a climax of sorts, although that takes up a further ten pages – which read, I found, much more quickly than the twenty five preceding them. And then there is a three page diminuendo. The structure is reminiscent of the novella, and at forty pages 'short story' seems a questionable description. The turning point, which a classic novella would demand, comes as less of a surprise than a relief.

The story needs that slow build up, because the young girl's vision of the window is slowly overwhelming her grasp on reality. It is becoming an obsession. First she sees the window, then through it, then the furniture of the room beyond. Finally she see a figure, that of a man, incessantly writing at his escritoire.

At this point the aunt, and the kindly Mr Pitmilly, intervene, taking the girl across the road to see 'the window' from the inside. This is the climactic, not moment, but scene. She finds out that indeed the window is not a window, but the mere facade of one, behind a bookcase. She runs back to her aunt's house, where she sees the window again, and the man, and what's more he opens the window and waves to her, before disappearing. A street boy has seen also, not the man, but the window standing open, but the vision is over.

Her aunt finally explains, that the women of their family are cursed to see this figure, for their ancestors have killed him for having an illicit, but unspecified relationship with their sister. The final three pages of the story tell of the rest of the girl's life, during which she hopes to see again, the ghostly man. Perhaps she does, but the blight of the curse is brought home to us in the penultimate paragraph, and in a succinct few words that capture a lifetime:

'home a widow from India, very sad, with my little children'

This sad homecoming is where she thinks she's sees the man again. He waves to her from the crowd, amongst which there is no one to meet her, but he does not go on to meet her either, and the story ends a half page later with her musing on what her aunt has told her and in recalling the 'Library Window.'

The story in its structure reminds me of Hemingway's *A Canary For One*. The differences are much greater, but one similarity is that use of a descriptive build up to a revelation, and a build up which, though a tenth the length of Oliphant's, seems, until we know its significance, almost as tedious.

In fact, I wonder to what extent the sheer number of words in Oliphant's story is the result of the need to tell the story, or of the need to fill a leisured readership's hours. Hensher asserts that the short story works best between 4,000-7,000 words in length, a contention that I find hard to accept. Certainly, if I were to select my top hundred stories, from any source, I would not expect to find many of them exceeding by much his lower margin.

I wonder too if there has been a tightening of storytelling over the last two hundred years, much as there has been over the hundred years of story showing in the film genre. The rise of popular printing, and reading, as opposed to listening to tales, could well have resulted in longer stories being produced. The printing itself not only frees the writer from the constraints of the listener's patience and the teller's memory, but also might have required more explanatory texts for a relatively un-sophisticated readership.

If we look at voiced readings today, the five minute, ten minute, and, pushing it, fifteen minute short story sets the limit, and that makes a maximum of around 2,200 words. Competitions and small magazines have often a similar upper limit. Nowadays, and certainly for me, the 4,000 and upwards short story seems heavy, and overlong.

Oliphant's striking portrait of a failing life though, in those quoted eleven words, is as punchy and effective, and short, as any one might expect to find today, more so than most. The drawn out lead up, like the long slow pull up a featureless mountain slope, only serves to heighten the impact of the final view. Except, that Oliphant's final view comes later, and is less impactful. It is more like one of those 'minor keys' that George Moore said all 'great stories' end in.

There is a sadness pervades this story, which seems rooted in more than just the growing revelation of the ghostly curse laid upon the family of women. There is a sense of disappointment and frustration throughout, and one that centres on the connection between men and women, and the fulfilment of their relationships.

The story is told by the young girl: it is a first person narrative, and as she builds the picture of the man behind the window, she draws repeatedly on memories of her father. Apart from Pitmilly, and the street boy, and the ghost, there are no male characters in the story, and even Pitmilly is a failed lover of the aunt. There are men missing, and palpably so, from this story, as there were from Oliphant's life. Their loss, their failures to consummate and sustain the relationships with the women of the cursed family, especially Aunt Mary herself, and her relative, Lady Carnbee (who wears a ring, passed at her death to the narrator, that was the never explained 'token', presumably of the murdered man) are the hidden story behind the ghost. The repeated 'imagination is a great deceiver' seems to refer, not just to the window, and its visions, but to life itself.

It is a story about disappointed expectations.

8 A.E.COPPARD'S 'MY HUNDREDTH TALE'

A.E.Coppard's *My Hundredth Tale* is one of the ten tales in *Nixey's Harlequin*, his seventh collection.

It's a long story, and episodic, that quality being emphasised by its being given numbered segments, like some of the longer D.H.Lawrence short stories. Cast in the first person, this tale purports to be the autobiography of John Flyn. This character is seen by many, including I suspect, Coppard himself, as the literary alter-ego of the author. Many writers have such dopplegangers: James Joyce has his Stephen Daedalus. Hemingway has his Nick Adams. Dickens has David Copperfield. These are not merely authorial mouthpieces, like Roth's Nathan Zuckermann; convenient devices for narrating a story, indeed, in Joyce's case, the character does no narrating at all, but is observed by an unseen author – the one that refined himself out of existence – though observed from the inside as well as the out.

Alter-egos are slightly, or perhaps profoundly different. Johnny Flyn is much more closely bound to his maker, I suspect, than is Zuckermann. One has to know only a little about Coppard's own life to begin to wonder just how closely the events of Flyn's are modelled upon them. And after the events come the feelings that the character expresses about the events. Johnny lives in poverty, with a tailor who dies young, for a father and with a mother who brings up her family single handed. Johnny becomes a runner, as did Coppard, and he goes to live in a cottage in the woods – perhaps the most famous thing that Coppard did, apart from write stories. Oh, yes, and Johnny writes too. Unlike Coppard, Johnny is a novelist, his first called *The Immortal Target*, which might possibly be the one that this short story is aiming at.

What makes this rambling story so readable, is the fact that the insights we are shown, into Johnny's behaviour, into the processes of self-awareness, into the way that relationships develop and founder, are so striking; and by that I do not mean merely noticeable. They strike at our own complacencies, and our own sensitivities. If you haven't done, or said, or felt any of the painful things in this story – you should become a politician.

My Hundredth Tale seems like a novel, more than a short story, more than a tale. Yet, tales can be long, longer than most tails, one imagines. They can be shaggy dog stories. It was reading about the writer George Moore that first made me stop and think about the autobiographical in fiction in relation to my own work. I think I'd got hold of the idea that it was somehow grubby and second rate – not really creative in fact – to use one's own life as the basis for story. Some of us get these daft ideas when we are kids (especially, if, unlike Coppard, we've had the benefits of a protracted state education).

Moore plundered joyfully his own life and the lives of those about him in the creation of his fictions. Then he plundered his booty, mixing and matching from tale to tale: lifting shorts out of novels, and incorporating into novels shorts he'd published elsewhere. Well, of course he did. Why wouldn't he? It was a revelation to me.

There's also the fact that there's nothing else really in there, that putty-filled dome that wobbles on the top of your vertebrae: there's what you've experienced. First hand, second hand, third hand and umpteenth hand. And much of it has been so mashed up, mixed and mashed, and mis-interpreted, and filed under the wrong headings, and corrupted by frequent copying and other metaphors, that when it does squeeze out, even the most discerning of us might be forgiven for thinking that we had made it up, out of thin air!

We use one set of experiences to explore the ideas, and feelings, that another set gave us. We twist, turn, transpose and translate (thought I'd only get three there...but sometimes it goes well!) what we have been, into what our characters might become. In this way truths are caught in the net of lies that we call fiction. The title *My Hundredth Tale* is itself a curiosity, drawing attention, as it does, to the author, rather than to any content of the tale. The number has a significance that is apparent, and perhaps relevant, only to the author. Who else is counting? Who else would think that way-marker worth noting? Who else, of course, would be passing it? Among the few and obscure references one has to search through to get a critical second opinion on Coppard, I've come across the assertion that when he first published, in 1919, he already had a 'shed full' of stories. As someone with a similar quantity on ice, I'm fairly certain that they wouldn't have been published in the order they were written. Was his hundredth tale, I wonder, the hundredth written, or the hundredth published, and which of those two markers should we take as being the genuine way-mark of a writer's journey? In fact, if you count up the titles in the main collections, this tale is eighth in the seventh volume, which makes it his ninety first published story. Unless of course, he's counting magazine and journal publications, which throws everything into doubt.

Johhny Flyn's autobiography, which is what this purports to be, is a soul searching affair, in which self doubt, even self-loathing, seems to trump the nuggets of self-awareness that the story throws up. Beginning with the narrator's relationship with his parents, it passes through a rivalry with a contemporary male friend, into a period of what we might these days call promiscuity, and on to several specific relationships, all of which founder for reasons of pride and personal, rather than class, snobbery. In the voice of Johhny, Coppard identifies the loveless, detached life of the writer, falsifying and replicating the emotions he perceives in others, yet failing to experience them fully himself – a failure that he knows and understands only too well, but which he cannot correct, despite his epiphanies.

Some of those epiphanies come out in pithy one-liners:

"Things are never what they seem-they are merely what they are."

"a book like this, full of half-truths-truths as I see them, the other halves hidden from me yet so very plain to you."

"...I was a mere sponge that sucked up other people's tears and squeezed them out as my own..."

This is the soul searching not merely of a person, but of a person who is a writer, and early on in the story, he has been told the secret of what being a successful writer is:

"to write, and write authoritatively, about nothing."

The theory here, in case you might benefit from it, is that anything the reader finds in the writing will be credited to the author!

In Coppard's autobiography, *It's Me, O Lord*, he writes about the fictionalising of his life story, but what struck me, reading *My Hundredth Tale*, were the truths, about writing, about living in poverty, and about relationships, that could not be revealed in a factual account without seeming, well, rather self-indulgent, and perhaps even false. If this tale was indeed the hundredth written, or, which may be more likely, was given that title to add the significance of a milestone to the content, it is ironic that it should appear in the collection that many see as marking the turning point in Coppard's canon. The collection *Nixey's Harlequin*, its gaudy covers hidden by a discreetly plain dust jacket, was published in 1931, a dozen years after his first. The following six collections would be spread over sixteen years, of what most commentators have seen as a decline.

That decline might have been only in what was published. There are gems in the later collections, but Coppard was running out of steam, or that shed was getting empty. There is no other title to follow that seems such a way-marker of the writer's progress. Does that tell us something about his perception of his own trajectory? I count another hundred and five published tales in the collections still to come, at least one of them about Johnny Flyn, but none is entitled 'My Two Hundredth Tale.' Perhaps by the time a writer gets that far he, or she, has done with way-markers, or perhaps I've been reading too much into the title of his ninety first story.

[further essays on Coppard by Mike Smith can be found in *English of the English*, which is available on Amazon for Kindle, or as a print book]

9 'THE MURMURING FOREST' BY VLADIMIR KOROLENKO

It's difficult today, in Britain, even in the wilds of Scotland to get yourself deep enough into a forest to not be able to see out to moorland or farmland; impossible, almost, to get yourself deep enough in to be unable – in the right direction – to walk out in a few hours. But in the forests of Poland, and the Ukraine you can still get into forests too big to get around, too big to get out of without a slice of luck, or magic, or heroism. These must have been the forests that Vladimir Korolenko was imagining, and remembering, when he wrote his story, *The Murmuring Forest*, which can be found in the Folio Society's *Russian Short Stories* (1997).

Korolenko was a late nineteenth century writer of Polish-Ukranian descent, and though he did most of his writing under the Tsars, he lived, and wrote into the Revolutionary period, dying in 1921. His tale has the quality of a folk tale, but beneath its archetypes there lurk real people, and the structure of his story – three asymmetric parts to make up around 8,000 words – emphasises this aspect. The forest is not only a race-memory, but also a metaphor for anywhere that human stories 'take place,' and the qualities attributed to it in this story can be seen as qualities inhabiting all human societies and the places in which they have developed. Though Korolenko's forest 'murmurs' in the background, and is presented as having a will and taking action itself, it is human desires and fears, and personalities that drive the events of this story.

I was minded of the story again when my wife decided to throw out some old beer mats. One, advertising a Belgian bier called Kwak – which I've never encountered – had a scribbled note on the back. She passed it over. Those who have seen my notebooks will not be surprised that I had a job to decipher what I'd written, but it turned out to be a quotation from Korolenko's story:

> 'The truth in a fairy tale is like iron, having passed for many years from hand to hand and got rusted, while the truth in a song is like gold and never rusts.'

The assertion is made by the character 'Opanas', in the tale the old man tells of the forest to the young 'Pan' who narrates it to us.

Re-reading the story I found I had no recollection of it until quite close to the end. It begins with the narrator riding through the forest. It begins with what he wants us to know, and to feel, about it.

> 'The Forest Murmured.
>
> There was always a murmur in this forest, a prolonged,measured murmur, like the echo of distant bells, tranquiland mellow, like a soft song without words, like a hazy recollection of the past.'

Those opening two lines pre-empt the old man, Grandfather's later descriptions, and put into our minds the ideas both of 'song' and of recollection. How we see the forest, and the grandfather who lives in it, will influence our reaction to his tale. He is described as 'bald-headed,' and 'grey-whiskered,' and more importantly, as seeming to be 'trying to recall something.'

The narrator, whom the old man refers to as 'boy' invites a tale, but before he gets it the old man gives us his version of what the forest is. He begins by throwing doubt on his own powers of observation, and recollection: 'what could I see, boy?' 'I do not know whether I have lived in the world or not.'

It is an approaching storm that has driven the narrator to the old man's door, where also live Zakhar and Maxim, hunting companions of the narrator. They are away, with Motria – presumably their mother – searching for a lost cow. As the storm develops the old man talks, and the forest's murmur becomes a roar.

> '..the roar of the forest was borne along in a deep, rising chord.'

The old man talks of the savagery of the forest; an aspen is 'cracking and shaking,' a pine 'begins to roar and moan.' He tells of a 'master' too, who tries to uproot trees, and has threatened even him, 'nearly disfiguring my face.' 'The master of the forest is an abominable creature,' he says, but then 'Grandfather dropped his head and sat for a while in silence.' The moment has come for his memory to clear, and for his tale proper to begin.

There are several characters in his story all of which seem archetypal, yet also real. This is story about how people treat each other; about how they behave. The old man is remembering his childhood, an orphan given to the forester Roman, to live in this very hut. Overlord to them is 'the Pan,' who uses Roman cruelly, having him beaten into accepting a wife, Oksana, whom he does not want: 'I want to make you happy, fool.' The Pan's 'whipper-in' Opanas, wants Oksana, but that is not the Pan's wish. Opanas is also a musician, and will sing the song, later, that foretells what will happen to the Pan, at the hands of Roman.

The lives of these people are limited, brutal, violent, and yet touched with moments of compassion and tenderness. A child is born and dies, but Roman is not convinced that it was his. Then the Pan, and Opanas visit the hut, and the Pan tries to get Roman drunk. Opanas suggests to him that the Pan is after Oksana, and plots a murder.

It is this murder, after the Pan has rejected Opanas' warning song, that the old man has heard, out in the forest. As his tale ends, the storm rages, and he subsides into a sleepless stupor, in which he repeats his questions to Oksana when he was a child, hearing the murder. Now, it is Motria, returned with the two boys and the lost cow, who answers him, and the story ends with the storm breaking into rain.

The forest might dominate the story, but it is not what the story is about. The actions of the players, enabled, necessitated, by their rigid social relationships of abuser and abused are what the story is about, and care is taken to differentiate the now of the narrator's story, with that of the old man's reminiscence.

The structure of the story, a three way split into unevenly sized parts, emphasises differences of viewpoint between the generations, between then and now. The first section, roughly four pages, allows the narrator to establish his view, of the forest, and of the old man, and of the old man's view of the forest. The violence of the old man's forest, is in contrast to the 'tranquil and mellow' forest of the narrator. The middle section, some fourteen pages, in which the old man tells his story, lays out the way the people with whom he grew up behaved towards each other. The Pan beats Roman, who in turn ill-treats his patient wife. Opanas, the 'whipper-in' connives with Roman to murder the Pan, and then tries to warn the Pan in his song. The Pan rebukes him, and Opanas and Roman take revenge.

The final section, with the return of Zakhar and Maxim, and Motria, shows the old man in another light. As if enfeebled by his recollection, he becomes stupefied, but does not sleep. 'Who is that moaning in the forest?' and 'who is that firing in the forest?' he asks Motria, but he calls her Oksana, and we know that he is repeating exactly the questions he asked of Oksana in his story.

Though the term had not then been coined, the old man seems to be suffering from PTSD, and the story is as good a fictional example of what that means as perhaps any. It is murder he has heard as a child, which he recalls as an old man, projecting its violence on to the forest, and to its savage 'master.' The breaking rain that ends the narration, suggests the cathartic tears that the old man has been, and still is, unable to release.

'He forgets that Oksana has long departed' Motria tells the narrator.

It is curious that I had lifted from this story that quotation which I began with. To make, in a story, such a strong, and seemingly dismissive assertion about 'story' in comparison to song, seems perverse, and I wondered to what extent we are meant to take it at face value. Opanas has spoken it, whilst trying to persuade the Pan to take heed of the warning in the song he has just sung. But the Pan dismisses the suggestion: 'with us it is not so.'

Opanas gives one more, explicit warning, which is rejected: 'the Pan.....kicked the Cossack like a dog,' and then the die is cast. 'Opanas rose like a dark cloud and exchanged glances with Roman.' He then smashes his mandore (instrument).

The quotation still haunts me though, for it has the ring of meaning, if not of truth. Could that 'us' with whom 'it is not so,' be the same 'us' as are reading the story, and as are listening to it with the narrator? And might the way it is 'not so,' be that we value the rusted ironwork of story more than the un-rusted gold of songs?

The story, sub-titled 'A Polish Legend' is told by a Polish-Ukranian through a Russian narrator, in Russian, and to a Russian audience. The distancing of it being a non-Russian story – like a tale from the Mabinogion told to an Englishman – makes it tale of 'them' rather than 'us,' a storyteller's technique for getting us to consider unpalatable truths about ourselves.

10 THE STORIES OF FRANÇOIS COPPÉE (1842-1908)

Coppée is one of the French writers in volume 5 of Hammerton's The World's Thousand Best Stories, where he gets a generous half-page of introduction to himself. His reputation, it suggests, has always lagged behind his merit. The fact that he is one of the writers in the 1920 anthology, *The Twelve Best Short Stories in the French Language* was perhaps a step towards correcting that, but he doesn't make it into the Folio Society's *French Short Stories*.

There are five stories in the Hammerton, so six in all on my shelves, and they have a consistency of approach, style, and subject matter that gives a sense of the writer. All are relatively short, in comparison with other stories of their time running to four or five pages, and all are rather sentimental. I'm getting to that age where tears come more easily than they did, when there's a little bit of pathos in the air, and Coppée seems to turn out a reliably three-tissue story.

But why wouldn't one cry, when the subject matter is so often about the harsh realities of poverty, frustrated loves, and death? In *The Gold Coin* a child freezes to death while a gambler wins a fortune. In *Died at Sea*, a young girl braids her air to the seaweed, knowing that she cannot escape the rising tide, but wanting to ensure that her body will be found for burial. In *The Gate Keeper*, a disappointed young Queen, whose husband has turned out to be a vile lecher, learns, from the eponymous hero whose wife has abandoned him and their baby, the importance of bringing up her son to be a better man than his father. In *An Accident*, a man confesses to a murder than we cannot fail to want him to receive forgiveness for.

All Coppée's stories seem to carry this theme of hardship and difficulty being set against morality, yet he has that lightness of touch that makes French storytelling sparkle so. In *The Gate Keeper*, the young Queen travels by train in the company of a Baroness, and a General. The general is not so much satirized as humanized, by the fact that his hobby, or passion even, is knitting.

> 'the general, in despair, has left a magnificent bedspread behind him that he was busy knitting for his daughter-in-law, taking nothing with him to beguile the tedium of the journey but material for a modest pair of worsted stockings.'

There's a gentle laughter, rather than a scorn, called for her, I think, and when we learn that on arrival at Paris 'he will betake himself without delay to a certain wool-shop in the Rue Saint-Honoré' we are expected to like him all the more for it! Like all the stories I have read by this author, this one invites us to contemplate serious issues, rather than harshly to be confronted by them.

'That was before the rising had overthrown her parents' thrown; and she loved the calm, sleepy atmosphere of the little court of Olmutz, where etiquette was tempered with homeliness.'

Her acceptance, following a romantic proposal in a flower arbour, is described with subtle irony:

> ' ...repressing with one hand the mad beating of her heart, "Yes, Sire!"

while the furious violins of the Hungarians attacked all together the

first notes of the Czech March, that sublime song of enthusiasm and triumph!'

Within a few lines though, 'a brutal chance had informed her that she had been deceived'. She ponders upon this tragedy, while the train that his carrying her to Paris, for respite with her mother, is stopped at a wayside halt. It will be there, the guard informs them, for an hour or two. The night is bitterly cold. 'all Europe is covered with snow,' and 'the foot warmers are cold.'

The general, 'divines that now is the moment to be heroic,' in which observation I find that French lightness of touch, the rap of a folded fan upon your shoulder! He 'jumps down to the rails, sinks knee-deep in the snow' and finds that there is a Gate-Keeper's house, with a fire. The royal party descends, and goes inside, to where a typical Coppée character, the Gate-Keeper 'has kept on his goatskin, kneels in front of the fire and puts dead wood on the fire-dogs.'

'It is a peasant's room.' And the Queen takes it all in, her eye falling finally on the cradle in the corner, wherein the man's three-year old daughter lies asleep. In a crucial exchange the Queen learns something that will cast her situation into a new light.

'.....her mother?" Her Majesty asks with some hesitation, and, as the man shakes his head, "you are a widower?"

But he makes another sign of negation.'

His wife has fled, to live a debauched life in the city. Gate-Keeper and Queen are in a similar situation, but there is one great difference, which she, and we, perceives.

'....I will never part from her..never, not even for an hour!"

"But why?"

"Why?" the man answered in a sad tone. "Because I will trust no one but myself to make the child what her mother has not been.....'

The Gate-Keeper is then called away to his duties, and for an hour the Queen rocks the cradle. Finally the snow is cleared from the line – it has been the right kind of snow, I think – and the royal party completes its journey. The story ends by telling us (not showing!) that the Queen, who has left a purse of gold for the Gate-Keeper's child is scarcely ever absent from her son's side now, and that whenever they see a Gate-Keeper on their travels, 'the royal child.......throws him a kiss.'

The sentimentality of the story is undeniable, but so is its integrity, and its truths. Interestingly, it is written in the present tense, which leaves us, curiously, at the end of the story, looking back on it!

The equally sentimental *Died at Sea*, prompted, Hammerton's introduction suggests, by 'half a dozen words concerning a Breton superstition' strikes a similar balance. It a simple story too, in which a fisherman dies at sea, leaving his daughter to be brought up by a family friend. The superstition is that if the body is not buried on land, the soul will not rest till judgement day. Only the women of the community harbour this belief, and the daughter grieves for her father's soul, for though his shipmates' bodies came ashore, his did not. The family friend tells the story to an old seamen who has found the gravestone of the girl whilst out walking, It is the seaman, in a classic example of 'framing,' who has set the scene for us, and is accosted by the storyteller at the graveside. When she goes alone to seek for shellfish on the shore and she is cut off by the tide, it is her courage, in preparing for death that impresses the teller of the story. She has tied down her skirts, for modesty, and fastened her hair to the seaweed on the rocks where she will drown. The story ends 'Oh! Brave people of the sea! Oh! Noble Brittany!' This is not merely a rousing close, but what the story is truly about.

A harsher story, but arguably no less sentimental, is *An Accident*, in which a workman appears at provincial confessional box after twenty five years of living in Paris. The bored Abbé, expecting the usual trite and trifling confession, is astounded to hear that he is confessing a murderer. What is told, is, in effect, a life story. It is one of two friends, the one cleverer than the other, who go to Paris for work. The penitent is the duller of the two, but steady. He sends the money he earns, little enough, back to his mother whom he is supporting. The other, who is brighter, and earns much more, spends it on the high life. The penitent falls in love and proposes to his landlady's daughter, but then introduces her to his friend, who – to quote Doctor John – 'steals her away.' The penitent accepts all this with remarkably good will, remaining a family friend and becoming a godfather to their child. But as life rolls on, the marriage sours. The bright one continues to waste his money, and to carry on with other women. The penitent helps out when he can, and remains a true friend.

Then the son is called up for military service, which means that he will no longer be able to help his mother. She will be abandoned to the unfaithful, feckless, and by now drunkard father. This is what precipitates the murder – for the son of a widow would be exempt from service.

When the tale is told the man asks for forgiveness. We are not told whether or not he gets it, but he has given a cross, that was to have been the betrothal present to the mother of his godson, to be sold for alms. The Abbé, putting into the poor-box money equal to its value, has kept it, and the story ends with him praying to it, for the soul of the man.

This is quite a modern story, in the sense of not coming to a decisive end, but leaving us to ponder on what will, and perhaps what ought, to happen to that soul, if there is such a thing!

Two other stories make up the half dozen that I have read by Coppée. These are *The Miracle* and *The Substitute*. Quite different in their content, they have, to my ear, a striking similarity of tone, and purpose. The former is a Christmas story, in which a rich man's neglected, but spoiled child is 'lost,' only to be found by a poor man, who takes him in. The distraught father, beginning to recognise the error of his ways, goes to collect his son, asleep beside the child of the poor man, in a room where shoes have been set out, to receive the gifts of Christmas night. The rich man sees beyond his own life, and vows that the two boys will share the toys he has bought for his son, but more, 'you have also reminded me, who am rich and lived only for myself, that there are other poor who need to be looked after. I swear by these two sleeping children, I won't forget them any longer.'

The Substitute, though quite a different story, has a similar moment of individual personal realisation, and taking of responsibility. Here, a lifelong criminal, driven to rather than choosing his way of life, but in the process of rehabilitation, offers himself in the place of a young man who is beginning on the road that the eponymous hero has already taken. The authorities are only too willing to believe that he is the guilty one, and the story ends: 'Today he is at Cayenne, condemned for life as an incorrigible.' In saving his friend, Jean Francois, has sacrificed his freedom, but completed his redemption.

These hard stories always carry the promise that we may redeem ourselves, but always at the cost of sacrifice of what we have held dearest. The sentimentality is built on a fierce, passionate belief in the principles that it asserts.

11 'THE CURSE OF IGAMOR' BY MICHAEL DE LARRABEITI

I've written about the late Michael De Larrabeiti's *Provencal Tales* before, but one in particular seemed worthy of a closer look. That is *The Curse of Igamor*.

It's one of those stories that combine those twins pillars of story, form and content, in such a way that one does not know which to deal with first. Content is what story is about, and briefly, this story is about a wicked Lord who, in the pursuit of higher taxes, intimidates the population of his town with that eponymous curse. Igamor is a magical horse, that if touched only even briefly by a human, binds that human to it, and carries him away, to be devoured.

The town is called Aigues Mortes – which seems to me to suggest 'pain of death.' A troubadour visits the town, once a friendly and hospitable place for troubadours, but finds a cold welcome. Undaunted he sits in the square, and, guarded by watchmen at the four corners – in case the Lord's soldiers show up – he tells, at night, a tale to ease the burden of hunger and fear that lies upon the inhabitants. He tells the story of 'this very town,' 'threatened with the curse of Igamor.'

As with all stories, where form and content are successfully combined, the content reveals the form, and the form supports the content, as can be seen here, even in the very opening of the story.

Of course, the story that the troubadour tells, is that of a troubadour appearing in the town, and finding it 'so cheerless' that he 'gathered them together and began to tell them a story.' And, in that story too, it is the curse of Igamor which the town has been threatened with.

The people question the troubadour: 'what good does it do to go round and round in the same place?' and the troubadour answers, 'It does little good.' Then he tells the story a different way, in which a monkey belonging to the troubadour in the story, slips away from the square, just as his own monkey is doing as his story is being told.

The monkey has made its way to the Lord's apartment, and filled his sleeping mind with images of riches, brought by sea, and which it will be his to claim, if he can get there before his Chancellor, and his Magician, who have made a pact to rob him of these riches.

The monkey, of course, has planted the tale in the minds of the other two as well, and all three hasten to their doom, each finding a horse waiting for him outside, each leaping onto the horse. Each finding that he has mounted the cursed Igamor.

In the troubadour's story, the people of the town awake next morning to find the troubadour singing and playing his lute loudly in the square. Their fears have been banished, and joy returns to the town.

The citizens have enjoyed the story, and go to their beds wondering if it might come true for them. After all, their troubadour had a monkey, just like the one in the story. And in the morning, Mellano – that is the troubadour's name – is singing and playing his lute loudly in the square.

But the soldiers come for him, and the townspeople are beaten back as he is taken away.

There is one last set of circles to be revealed. A young man, the bravest in the town, comes out to find the beaten body of Mellano, with his broken flute beside him, and the monkey Heloise nearby. He asks the troubadour, why the story did not come true for his town? Because not enough of you believed it, Mellano tells him.

"Are you often flogged?' asked the young man.

'Often,' answered Mellano,'

Perhaps more potently, Mellano tells him also, that he does not know, when he sings and plays each morning after telling his tale, whether enough people will have believed it, and thus made it come true, or whether, as in the story De Larrabeiti has told, they will not, and he will be whipped.

The young man says that he too would like to become a troubadour, but Mellano tells him to stay in his own town, and to help his own people to remember, and to believe the story. He, Mellano, must go on to tell it, and be flogged, elsewhere.

I like the structure of this story, its circles within circles. It reminds me of a poem called *Ring Song*, by Pete Morgan, which is on a similar theme, of stories being passed on. But De Larrabeiti's tale carries this extra element, that of the role of the storyteller in the ongoing struggle between order and chaos, structure and freedom; between belief in what should be believed, and in what should not. The townspeople are oppressed because they believe in their Lord's Igamor, but not in their own. Mellano must suffer for his story, and it must be a story worth suffering for, and the young man who speaks to him, must keep its memory alive. De Larrabeiti has told a tale that, though rooted in a medieval past, is as fresh, and as pertinent today as it was then, and it is a tale that challenges us, as writers, to consider how far down Mellano's road we ourselves would be prepared to walk.

[Provencal Tales was published in 1988 by St.Martin's Press, New York, and second hand copies can be found on the web.]

12 'THE MISFITS' BY ARTHUR MILLER

American writer Arthur Miller is best known for his plays, and in the case of *The Misfits*, probably for his screenplay. The 1961 John Huston film though, was based on Miller's short story of the same name, dated to 1957 in the 2009 *Presence, Collected Stories* (Bloomsbury).

There is lot of documentation and testimony regarding the film adaptation. The story of the filming is as epic as the film itself and carries echoes of the short story's themes. Huston is said to have been addicted to gambling. His male lead, Clark Gable, pushed himself to the limits, and died a fortnight after filming finished. Marilyn Monroe was moving towards divorce from Miller, and she too died less than two years after the film was released. Montgomery Clift was said to be already experiencing problems with addiction.

Perhaps to cope with his unravelling marriage, Miller was rewriting the screenplay as the filming took place, adding more and more to the role that Monroe was cast in. In that sense the original story was progressively being left behind. Yet the short story remains the starting point for the film, and what remains of it, as well as what was removed, and added to it, can still hold the interest of the student of adaptation, and of story.

In several respects the short story is a much tighter construction. It takes place almost entirely within sight of the truck that belongs to the main character, Gay Langland, and that truck remains within the few square miles of Nevada desert where the three cowboys are hunting their wild horses. Only in the last page, when the cowboys have driven off towards the nearby town, does the story linger, and close, out in the desert, with the four tethered mustangs, and the colt.

It is not so much the addition of other places however, that marks the biggest change between text and film. That comes in the shape of Marilyn Monroe, for the character she plays in the film, exists in the short story only in the thoughts and words of the two protagonists, Gay, and Perce Howland. Guido, the third cowboy, does not refer to or think about her.

Here is one of the clear cut differences between the shown story of the film, and the told story of the word. For in the film Roslyn exists in her own right. In the text, it is the perceptions of her, harboured by others that we are told about. Our guess, which may be better than theirs, is all we have of the 'real', imagined character. The presence of the shown Roslyn, with her own words, her own actions, and her own observable character traits, tips the balance of the story, away from the relationship between Gay and Perce, towards the relationships between each of them, and her.

In his introduction to the Bloomsbury collection – taken from the much earlier *'I Don't Need You Anymore'* (Viking, 1967) in which *The Misfits* was included – Miller makes several observations about the short story form, and also, at least by implication, about the film. Telling us that a short story tries to 'catch wonder by surprise' might give us a clue as to what we should look for, but more useful might be his assertion that the 'great strength of a good short story' is 'to see things isolated in stillness'. He writes at length too about dialogue: '..when the author...stopped chattering and got out of the way;' These three snippets alone would give us a reasonable approach to *The Misfits* in its text form, and one from which to view the diverging road to the film version.

Before looking at some examples in detail, one other general point might be useful, which is that there is a difference between the way that metaphors in text, and those in film work. In film we observe, or hear, the actual sight or sound on which the metaphor is built. If the roar of an engine does not sound to us like a growl, then the metaphor isn't brought into being. In the short story, the wheels of the light aircraft with which Guido chases the wild horses out of the mountains have 'doughnut tires.' How many of us, I wonder, would think of that when we see the tyres of the movie's plane? That this is a story full of metaphor suggests much risks being lost in the adaptation.

The most obviously powerful scene of the short story, for me, is where the stallion is brought to the ground. Unlike the other mustangs this one is not neatly roped and hog-tied and tethered.

'The stallion's forefeet slipped back, and he came down on his knees and his nose struck the clay ground and he snorted as he struck, but he would not topple over and stayed there on his knees as though he were bowing to something, with his nose propping up his head against the ground and his sharp bursts of breath blowing up dust in little clouds under his nostrils.'

He goes down stubbornly, slowly and with a sort of dignity,

resisting until the very end, when Gay 'came up alongside the stallion's neck and laid his hands on the side of the neck and pushed,...'

In the film, Perce frees the stallion, to please Roslyn who is present in the desert. Gay recaptures it, in the scene that may well have triggered Gable's fatal heart attack less than two days after filming ended. This is the most action packed scene of the film, in which Gable was dragged, apparently behind the horse, but in fact behind a vehicle, for a distance of several hundred feet. Despite the padding, he was severely cut and bruised, and it's said that he told his wife that it had been 'an accident.' Like the character he was playing though, Gable had made a choice; his being not to use a stand-in. His character then releases the stallion, telling Roslyn that he wanted to make his own decisions. Such a sequences would have no place in the textual story, and would in fact, undermine the essential metaphor of the piece, that the mustangs, whatever they are, cannot escape their fate, and neither can the cowboys. It is ironic, perhaps, that the actor in reality, was playing a role nearer to that of the character in the original story, than is the character he was portraying in the film.

There are nuances of dialogue and thought in the told story, especially where Gay recognises the futilities of his life, and the inevitability of his choosing them. Like the colt, trapped by its dependence, though un-tethered, by the side of its mother, Gay is tied to the futilities of his own life. Perce too is trapped, and even as they recognise their situation, they support each other's denial of it.

Gay's sense of freedom is compromised by his dependence on the truck.

'Gay owned the truck and he wanted to preserve the front end.'

'The transmission fork was worn out, he knew, and the front tires were going too.'

'The time was coming fast when he would need about fifty dollars or have to sell the truck, because it would be useless without repairs. Without a truck and without a horse he would be down to what was in his pocket.'

At that moment, he has precisely four silver dollars, given to him by Roslyn. He has been taking money from her, for doing odd jobs and driving her around. She is an 'Eastern' woman, of means, in the short story. The film avoids the issue, having Gay and Roslyn restoring a house together. The dependence experienced in the short story irks Gay, and when Perce refers to it, his reaction is instinctive:

'he felt angry blood moving into his neck.'

There Is a deeper irritation though, which is the knowledge that his way of life is mistaken, and ineffective. He uses the younger man to help maintain the denial of this truth.

'"Well, it's better than wages."

"Hell, yes."'

This exchange, and variations on it, is repeated more than once, as both men struggle to avoid acknowledging their situation, which is comparable to that of the horses they are pursuing. In fact, this is made explicit, for they refer both to themselves, and to the horses as 'misfits.' In the end though, it is an inescapable truth. Even the money they will make from the mustangs is poor: 'there would be no way to explain it so it made sense,'. For the much younger Perce, the truth is held further at bay, which is how he can support Gay in the delusion. Even when he wins big prize money at the rodeo, Perce has no sense of needing to hang on to it: 'the boy was buying drinks for everybody with his rodeo winnings...'

Perce likes Gay because he 'never thought to say he ought to be making something of his life.' There is no suggestion, that I can see, that Perce understands in the slightest that Gay cannot make such a suggestion, because his own life demands that he remains in denial of such ideas.

All three of the short story's cowboys could have 'done better' in that traditional sense, but have turned down the chance, opting instead for a freedom as fragile, and ephemeral as that enjoyed by the mustangs they have captured.

Perce, though, already knows his fate: 'I'm never going to amount to a damned thing.' As he allows Gay to convince him that this is acceptable, Gay needs Perce to do the same for him. They are at opposite ends of the same journey. When Gay tells Perce that the colt would not be saved, even if left to run free, because 'He'd just follow the truck right into town' if the mare were on it, we recognise it as a metaphor for their own compulsions. The Roslyn of this story 'razzes' them on their way of life, but cannot save them from it, though the implication is that somewhere soon, she will save herself. Certainly Gay is conscious of holding himself ready for that: 'you never kept anything...' 'She would go back East one day, he knew, maybe this year, maybe next.'

This short story is one of those that sticks in the memory, because the more closely you read it the more you find in it, deepening, and refining the message it carries. Rather than pick out quotations here and there to support a point, one should be taking it line for line and explaining how each adds to the context in which we will understand what follows. The ending that the film works towards is not so much a consummation of that context, as a subversion of it, as Roslyn and Gay recognise the opposite of what the Gay of the short story recognises, and ride off into a Hollywood sunset together.

In the short story, it is Perce, the fellow-loser, whom Gay needs to make his future with.

'"You comin' up to Thighbone with me, ain't you?"

"Okay," Perce said and went back to sleep.

'Gay felt more peaceful now that the younger man would not be leaving him. He drove on in contentment.'

This is the happy ending that Susan Lohafer might find if she looked here for one of her 'anterior' endings. Three asterisks separate it from the page that follows, for it is not going to be Miller's ending. He takes us back to the desert, where the horses have been left. His description of them is our extended metaphor for the situation of his cowboys, and its end is focussed on the plight of that colt, which will make what we know will be a fatal choice. Reading the Wickipedia entry for Miller, there is a reference to him asserting that circumstances drive the choices of his characters. Gay, and Perce, and Guido, act as if they were like the colt, beyond rational choice, but Miller is pointing up the human tragedy, which is that we are not beyond it, but only incapable through our own natures. The film cannot go this far, and one wonders to what extent it was the genre, or the personal circumstances of the writer, or the requirements of the studios, that placed this limitation upon it.

The film makes explicit, not only the character of Roslyn, but also the wider context in which the protagonists' lives are lived. The memories that the short story Gay has, of bars and towns and rodeos, are made flesh, and are fleshed out with extra characters. His relationship with Roslyn is examined by that third person inquisitor, the camera, rather than by his thoughts and statements, about her, being eavesdropped upon by the reader. Perce and Guido too are shown in their interactions with her, rather than through the filters of memory, doubt and suspicions. In true Hollywood style, Roslyn is made significantly younger than Gay. In the story, we are told, she is 'about his age'. Hollywood men, and their audiences, were presumably incapable of dealing with women of their own age, and perhaps still are. In the film, Gay does not have to confront his ageing, though the actor was actually doing that, with lethal results. In the short story, the character contemplates turning 'forty six soon, and then nearing fifty' and getting grey hairs. Clark Gable, looking, and behaving, fitter than he was, had already turned fifty nine. In fact the film has increased the gap between Gay and Roslyn to a quarter century, pushing her back about fifteen years, and him forward nearly as many. This alone changes what the story can be about, as well as what it is.

In the short story Gay 'sensed the bottom of his life falling if it turned out Roslyn had really been loving the boy beside him'. In the film we see exactly what the relationship between Perce and Roslyn is, and her relationship with Guido is developed explicitly, from what, in the short story, is an equally explicit narrative denial: Thinking of the 'yearning for a woman', Guido is pleased that 'he was free of that..'

References made by the narrator, or in the thoughts of Gay, have to be shown. So we see him wanting to introduce his lost family to Roslyn, and becoming distraught when they vanish. But whereas, in the short story, these references are part of the context in which we consider his relationship with Perce, in the film, they relate to his relationship with Roslyn. Perce's home life is referred to by the narrator in the short story, but again, has to be made explicit in the film, in which we seen him talking to his mother in a phone kiosk. The camera cannot tell an internal story, but only show an external one.

The short story, in contrast, tells us the internal story and evokes in our imaginations the desert in which it takes place, and the images of the events and the players in them:

'A wild river of air swept and swirled across the dark sky and struck down against the blue desert and hissed back into the hills.'

'The jacket had one sleeve off at the elbow, and the dried leather was split open down the back, showing the lamb's-wool lining. He had bombed Germany in this jacket long ago.'

All these changes stem from the introduction of Roslyn as an actual, rather than as a 'thought about' character. From that first step the film has to move away progressively from the agendas of the short story. She draws the focus towards her, and changes what the story is revealing.

The final section of the film shoehorns in much of the action of the short story. The cowboys, with Roslyn tagging along, do go into the desert. Guido flies his beat-up old plane, and in his beat-up old flying jacket, to drive the wild mustangs out of the mountains and onto the plains, but the significance of his doing that is quite altered. He is no longer the device by which Perce and Gay get the time and opportunity to talk, and for Gay to think. A different role has to be found for him. He cannot be simply written out, for the plane is the means of getting the horses onto the plain! So he too, in direct opposition to his character in the short story, becomes romantically involved with Roslyn.

The character of Roslyn too, changes the agendas of the story. No longer imagined she has to be 'realised' by the author, and Miller, for reasons we can only speculate about, makes her childlike and vulnerable. She is not a character for whom going 'back East' would be an act of volition, so much as a running away. In that alone she changes the story's agenda, for Gay is not challenged, in his way of life, by her superior grip on it, as in the told story, but only in his ability to compromise in order to protect her from her own inadequacies. Her driving force seems to be an inability to accept the nature of life and death. In particular she has a rising revulsion against the hunt for the mustangs. An already over the top performance – her face barely stays still for a moment, but is constantly twitching and grimacing – leads to a wonderful temper tantrum in the desert, as spectacular as a four year old's in a mall! This precipitates the release of the captured horses, taking the shown story that final step away from the told one. Gay recaptures the stallion, exhausting both the fictional character, and the actor who portrays him, but then releases it, in a gesture of futile control, after which he and Roslyn ride off in to a Hollywood ending. The great differences are two-fold. The text has he and Perce make that exit. More importantly, the movie's horses are free, and there is no equivalent to that final page of Miller's original text, highlighting the metaphorical comparison with the misfit cowboys. In fact, at the end of the film it is hard to see either horses or men in that role. In the film, Clark Gable's character has retained his freedom, and so have the horses. Miller's short story was about him, and them, failing to do so.

John Huston was used to adaptation. His final film was a 'faithful' adaptation of James Joyce's *The Dead*, and is especially interesting for its closing sequence. There, Huston understood that he could do no better than have the final paragraphs of the short story read in voice over, while a shot lingers on a landscape similar to the one being described. This level of sensitivity to what is important to the story seems at odds with the changes wrought in *The Misfits*. Was that because, in this case, the adaptation was being driven by the changed agendas of the writer? Or was it something to do with Hollywood's need to present the stereotypical roles of man and woman? A character not even hinted at in the told story, is that of Roslyn's female sidekick, an older woman with a veneer of cynicism over a seam of old fashioned romance, and played with show-stealing enthusiasm by Thelma Ritter. Her function in the story is to tell us, repeatedly and explicitly, throughout the first half of the film, that 'cowboys' are real men, and thus OK, even if they have a propensity for vanishing. Once she has got this message clearly across, and, presumably, fixed in our heads, she is dropped from the story: job done!

The New York Times gave the film, on its release, a damning review. Its characters were shallow, it said, and its ending was sentimental. There is no hint that the reviewer knew of the short story that preceded it. My interest isn't to set one form above the other, nor to rate the success of an adaptation in relation to its 'fidelity' to the original, but to ask if the differences tell us anything about story and how it is used by storytellers.

The Misfits gives us a clear distinction, between a textual story, that examines the lives of, predominantly, two men, who are at different stages on the same road, and who use each other to avoid facing up to their failures, and an audio-visual one that strips the sense of failure from its male lead, and in fact validates that and other stereotypes by having him 'get' the girl in the end. In the former, the location, in time and place, and the events are used as a metaphor for the situations of the men. In the latter they become merely a visual accompaniment to the words and actions of the protagonists.

ABOUT THE AUTHOR

Mike Smith has published poetry, short plays and essays. His plays are available through Lazy Bee Scripts. He regularly writes for Thresholds, the International Post Graduate Short Story Forum. Writing as Brindley Hallam Dennis he has published several collections of short stories and a novella. His work has been widely performed and published in magazines, journals and anthologies. He lives in north Cumbria within sight of three mountain tops and a sliver of Solway Firth. He blogs at
www.Bhdandme.wordpress.com

The Broken Mirror (poetry)
No Easy Place (poetry)
Valanga (poetry)
Martin? Extinct? (poetry)
English of the English (essays on A.E.Coppard)
Readings for Writers Vol.1
The Poetic Image (a short course in the short story)

As Brindley Hallam Dennis
Second Time Around (short stories)
A Penny Spitfire (novella)
Talking To Owls (short stories)
Departures (short stories)
Ambiguous Encounters (short stories with Marilyn Messenger)
Ten Murderous Tales (short stories)
The Man Who Found A Barrel Full of Beer (short stories)

Printed in Great Britain
by Amazon